Babar
and the
Christmas House

Harry N. Abrams, Inc., Publishers

It was the middle of December, and Babar's four children were excited. They could almost smell Christmas in the air. Every day Pom, Flora, and Alexander, the oldest children, would walk to school and look at the decorations that had been put up on the houses.

Some of the houses had
beautiful wreaths on their doors.

Some houses had candles in their
windows. They glowed warmly and
invitingly at all who passed by.

But there was one house, way at the top of the biggest hill, that was different. This house had lots and lots of decorations on it.

The children didn't know who lived there. They had heard that someone new had moved in, but they had never seen these neighbors.

Each day it seemed that there was something new to look at. One day, a fantastic structure made of blinking lights appeared on the roof. It went up, up, up, almost to the sky.

Another day, it was an enormous sleigh with reindeer, perched right on top of the garage. The reindeer appeared to be made out of fruits and vegetables. Or maybe it was wood and cloth. It was hard to say.

Every day the children would go home and report to their parents on the progress of the incredible house.

"You have to go and see it!" Flora told Babar and Celeste. "You'll be amazed!"

"We will certainly have to go and see it soon," said Celeste.

Babar looked in his *Big Book of Celesteville Residents*. "Hmmm," he said. "Someone new lives there. We haven't met them yet."

A week before Christmas, a fountain appeared in the front yard of the amazing house. The water jetted up as high as the house, and little fishes played in the bubbles. Colored lights made the water look like a wonderful rainbow.

"I wonder who lives here," said Alexander.

The next day, Babar received a letter. It was from Rataxes, who was king of neighboring Rhino City. The elephants and the rhinos did not get along, so Babar was reluctant to open it.

"What does it say, my dear?" asked Celeste.

"Nothing good, I imagine," said Babar.

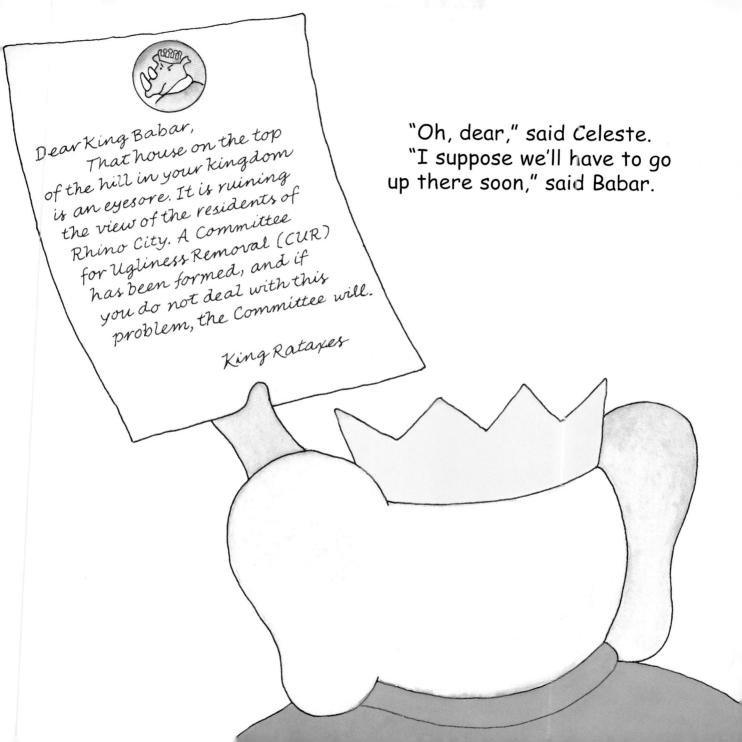

The next day, zillions of colored feathers had been added
to the house. The school had a field trip just to see it.

The following day, sparkly things had appeared, as well
as a large climbing tower festooned with colored lights.

"You must come and see the Christmas house!" said Pom, Flora, and Alexander.

And so, Babar and Celeste walked up to the top of the hill to see what all the fuss was about. Cornelius came too, and so did Isabelle, who was still too little for school.

"Well," said Babar. "This certainly is something."

"It certainly is something," said Celeste.

Just then, along came Rataxes and a number of other rhinos. "A-ha!" said Rataxes.

"A-ha!" said the CUR. "Are you going to do something about this?"

"Hmmm," said Babar.

Then the door of the house opened. Out came an elephant.
Another elephant was behind him.
   "Hello," said the elephant.
   "Hello," said Babar and Celeste.
The rhinos just scowled.

"I am Babar," said Babar. "This is Celeste. Welcome to Celesteville."

"How do you do?" said the elephant, bowing. "I am Hector, and this is my wife Hortense. We are very happy to be here. We have moved here from the other side of the mountains."

Rataxes stepped forward. "Explain yourself!" he said.
Hector looked puzzled. "What would you like me to explain?"
he asked.
"This . . . house!" said Rataxes.

Meanwhile, the children were playing in the fountain,
tickling each other with the feathers, and climbing on the tower.

"Ohh," said Hector. "The house. Well, you see, I am an artist, and this house is my Christmas gift to all of you."

"Aahh," said Babar. "So this is *art*."

"Of course," Hector replied.

"In that case," said Babar, "we thank you very kindly."

The rhinos frowned. They did not seem to know what to say.
"Well," said Rataxes finally, "if it's art . . ."
   ". . . I suppose there's nothing we can do about it," said the head of the CUR.
   "But we don't like it," said another member. And then they left.

The next day, the trees in front of the house were covered with balloons of many colors.

All of Celestville came and sang carols in the front yard, while the children batted the balloons back and forth. And when they were done, Hector brought out cider for everyone.

Designer: Becky Terhune

Library of Congress Cataloging-in-Publication Data

Brunhoff, Laurent de, 1925-
  Babar and the Christmas house / Laurent de Brunhoff.
     p. cm.
Summary: Newcomers to Celestville have so many Christmas decorations on
their hilltop house that Babar receives a demand from King Rataxes of
nearby Rhino City that the "ugliness" be removed.
  ISBN 0-8109-4583-5
  [1. Christmas decorations—Fiction. 2. Elephants—Fiction. 3.
Rhinoceroses—Fiction. 4. Kings, queens, rulers, etc—Fiction. 5.
Christmas—Fiction.] I. Title.

  PZ7.B82843Baad 2003
  [E]—dc21

                              2003001442

Conceived and developed by Harry N. Abrams, Incorporated, New York
Images adapted by Judith Gray, after characters created
by Jean and Laurent de Brunhoff
Text written by Ellen Weiss

Published in 2003 by Harry N. Abrams, Incorporated, New York

PRINTED AND BOUND IN HONG KONG

10 9 8 7 6 5 4 3 2 1

Harry N. Abrams, Inc.
100 Fifth Avenue
New York, N.Y. 10011
www.abramsbooks.com

Abrams is a subsidiary of
LA MARTINIÈRE
G R O U P E